CW00495079

Specimen Sight-Reading Tests for Baritone, Euphonium and Tuba 𝄢

Grades 6-8

**The Associated Board of
the Royal Schools of Music**

GRADE 6

BARITONE / EUPHONIUM

© 1998 by The Associated Board of the Royal Schools of Music

AB 2691

Baritone / Euphonium

GRADE 6

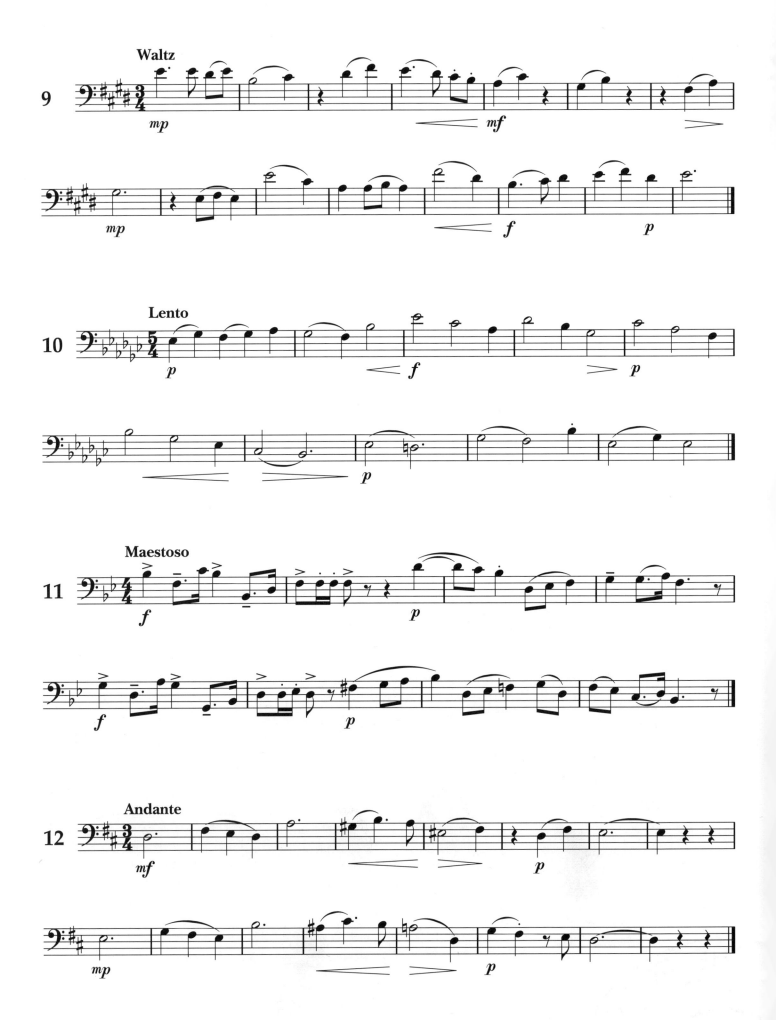

AB 2691

Baritone / Euphonium

Baritone / Euphonium

Baritone / Euphonium

GRADE 8

E♭ Tuba

C Tuba

F Tuba

Eb Tuba

Bb Tuba

C Tuba

3 Cantabile

F Tuba

1 Moderato

2 Vivo

3 Moderato

E♭ Tuba

GRADE 8

E♭ Tuba

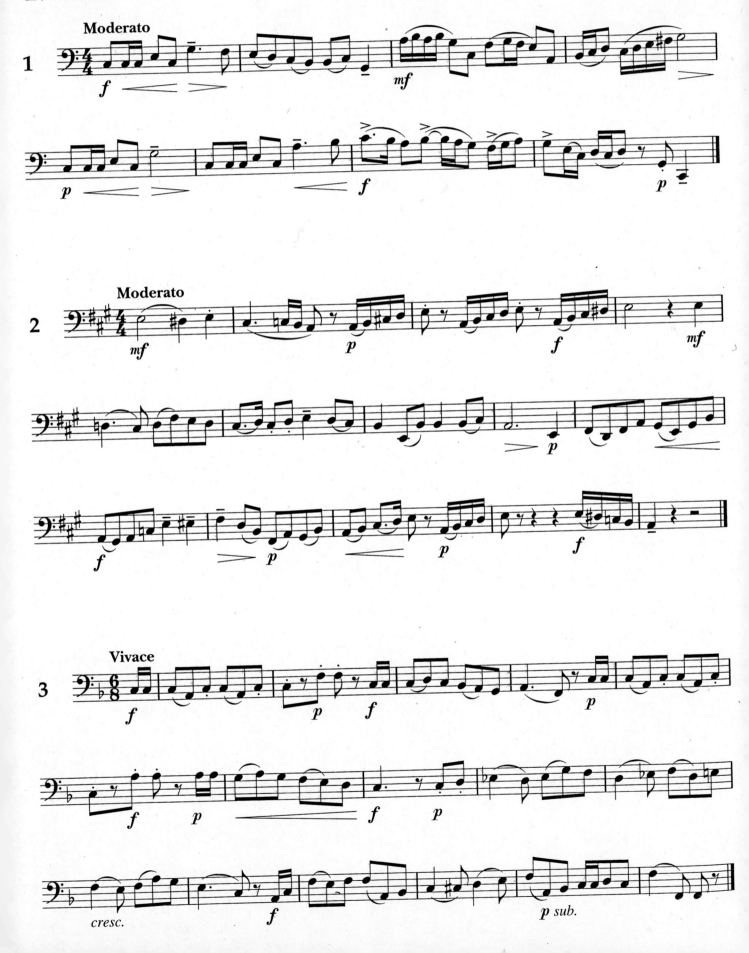

Tuba

B♭ Tuba

C Tuba

2

F Tuba

1

2

Printed and bound in Great Britain by Caligraving Limited